Sing a Song of
of
MOTHER GOOSE

BARBARA REID

North Winds Press
A division of Scholastic Canada Ltd.

Scholastic Canada Ltd.
123 Newkirk Road, Richmond Hill, Ontario, Canada L4C 3G5

Scholastic Inc.
730 Broadway, New York, NY 10003, USA

Ashton Scholastic Pty Limited
PO Box 579, Gosford, NSW 2250, Australia

Ashton Scholastic Limited
Private Bag 1, Penrose, Auckland, New Zealand

Scholastic Publications Ltd.
Holly Walk, Leamington Spa, Warwickshire CV32 4LS England

Art Director: Kathryn Cole

Photography: Ian Crysler

87654   Printed in Hong Kong   1234/9

Canadian Cataloguing in Publication Data

Mother Goose.
  Sing a song of Mother Goose

Issued also in French under title: Un, deux, trois, voilà la Mère l'Oie!

ISBN 0-590-71781-2

1. Nursery rhymes.   I. Reid, Barbara, 1957-
II. Title.

PZ8.3.M68Si 1987   j398'.8   C87-094259-X

A Diller, A Dollar

A diller, a dollar,
A ten o'clock scholar,
What makes you come so soon?
You used to come at ten o'clock,
But now you come at noon.

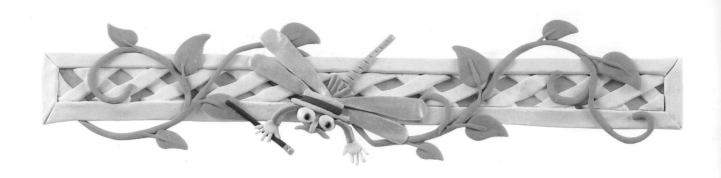

Ladybird

Ladybird, ladybird, fly away home!
Your house is on fire, your children all gone,
All but one, and her name is Ann,
And she crept under the pudding pan.

Georgie Porgie

Georgie Porgie, pudding and pie,
Kissed the girls
And made them cry;
When the boys
Came out to play,
Georgie Porgie ran away.

Thirty Days Hath September

Thirty days hath September,
April, June and November;
February has twenty-eight alone,
All the rest have thirty-one,
Excepting leap year, that's the time
When February's days are twenty-nine.

5

The Dogs Do Bark

Hark, hark,
The dogs do bark,
The beggars are coming to town;
Some in rags,
And some in jags,
And one in a velvet gown.

If

If all the world were apple pie,
And all the seas were ink,
And all the trees were bread and cheese,
What should we have for drink?

Baa, Baa, Black Sheep

Baa, baa, black sheep,
Have you any wool?
Yes, sir, yes, sir,
Three bags full;
One for the master,
One for the dame,
And one for the little boy
Who lives down the lane.

Sing A Song

Sing a song of sixpence,
A pocket full of rye;
Four and twenty blackbirds
Baked in a pie;

When the pie was opened
The birds began to sing;
Wasn't that a dainty dish
To set before the King?

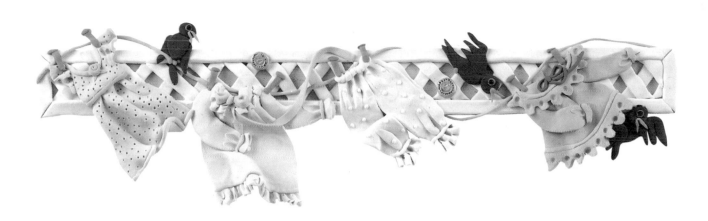

The King was in his counting house
Counting out his money;
The Queen was in the parlor
Eating bread and honey;

The maid was in the garden
Hanging out the clothes;
There came a little blackbird,
And snipped off her nose.

Jack a Nory

I'll tell you a story
About Jack a Nory,
And now my story's begun;
I'll tell you another
Of Jack and his brother,
And now my story is done.

Jack Be Nimble

Jack be nimble, Jack be quick,
Jack jump over the candlestick.

Hickory, Dickory, Dock

Hickory, dickory, dock,
The mouse ran up the clock.
The clock struck one,
The mouse ran down,
Hickory, dickory, dock.

One For The Money

One for the money,
Two for the show,
Three to get ready,
And four to go!

Jack And Jill

Jack and Jill
Went up the hill,
To fetch a pail of water;
Jack fell down
And broke his crown,
And Jill came tumbling after.

Little Boy Blue

Little Boy Blue,
Come blow your horn,
The sheep's in the meadow,
The cow's in the corn.
Where is the boy
Who looks after the sheep?
He's under a haycock
Fast asleep.
Will you wake him?
No, not I,
For if I do,
He's sure to cry.

Mary Had A Little Lamb

Mary had a little lamb,
Its fleece was white as snow,
And everywhere that Mary went
The lamb was sure to go.

It followed her to school one day,
Which was against the rules;
It made the children laugh and play
To see a lamb at school.

14

And so the teacher turned it out,
But still it lingered near;
It waited patiently about
For Mary to appear.

"Why does the lamb love Mary so?"
The eager children cried.
"Mary loves the lamb, you know,"
The teacher did reply.

15

Little Tommy Tucker

Little Tommy Tucker
Sings for his supper.
What shall he eat?
White bread and butter.
How will he cut it
Without e'er a knife?
How will he be married
Without e'er a wife?

Monday's Child

Monday's child is fair of face,
Tuesday's child is full of grace,
Wednesday's child is full of woe,
Thursday's child has far to go,
Friday's child is loving and giving,
Saturday's child works hard for a living,
And the child that is born on the Sabbath day
Is bonny and blithe, and good and gay.

17

Old King Cole

Old King Cole
Was a merry old soul,
And a merry old soul was he;
He called for his pipe,
And he called for his bowl,
And he called for his fiddlers three.

18

Here Is The Church

Here is the church and here is the steeple,
Open the doors and see all the people.
Here is the parson going upstairs,
And here he is saying his prayers.

Pat-a-Cake

Pat-a-cake, pat-a-cake,
Baker's man!
Bake me a cake
As fast as you can.
Pat it, and prick it,
And mark it with T,
Put it in the oven
For Tommy and me.

Pease Porridge

Pease porridge hot,
Pease porridge cold,
Pease porridge in the pot,
Nine days old.
Some like it hot,
Some like it cold,
Some like it in the pot,
Nine days old.

20

Little Jack Horner

Little Jack Horner
Sat in the corner,
Eating a Christmas pie;
He put in his thumb,
And pulled out a plum,
And said, "What a good boy am I!"

Old Mother Hubbard

Old Mother Hubbard
Went to the cupboard
To get her poor dog a bone;
When she got there
The cupboard was bare,
And so the poor dog had none.

22

She went to the baker's
To buy him some bread;
When she came back
The dog was dead.

She went to the undertaker's
To buy him a coffin;
When she came back
The dog was laughing.

She took a clean dish
To get him some tripe;
When she came back
He was smoking his pipe.

The dame made a curtsy,
The dog made a bow;
The dame said, "Your servant,"
The dog said, "Bow-wow."

Rain

Rain, rain, go away,
Come again another day;
Little Johnny wants to play.

Little Miss Muffet

Little Miss Muffet
Sat on a tuffet,
Eating her curds and whey;
There came a big spider,
Who sat down beside her
And frightened Miss Muffet away.

Hey Diddle, Diddle

Hey diddle, diddle,
The cat and the fiddle,
The cow jumped over the moon;
The little dog laughed
To see such sport,
And the dish ran away with the spoon.

Humpty Dumpty

Humpty Dumpty sat on a wall,
Humpty Dumpty had a great fall;
All the King's horses and all the King's men
Couldn't put Humpty together again.

Little Bo-Peep

Little Bo-Peep has lost her sheep,
And can't tell where to find them;
Leave them alone, and they'll come home,
And bring their tails behind them.

Pussy Cat, Pussy Cat

Pussy cat, pussy cat,
Where have you been?
I've been to London
To visit the Queen.
Pussy cat, pussy cat,
What did you there?
I frightened a little mouse
Under her chair.

Pins

See a pin and pick it up,
All the day you'll have good luck.
See a pin and let it lay,
Bad luck you'll have all the day.

Banbury Cross

Ride a cock-horse to Banbury Cross,
To see a fine lady upon a white horse.
With rings on her fingers and bells on her toes,
She shall have music wherever she goes.

Twinkle, Twinkle, Little Star

Twinkle, twinkle,
    little star,
How I wonder
    what you are!
Up above the world
    so high,
Like a diamond
    in the sky.

Solomon Grundy

Solomon Grundy,
Born on a Monday,
Christened on Tuesday,
Married on Wednesday,
Took ill on Thursday,
Worse on Friday,
Died on Saturday,
Buried on Sunday.
This is the end
Of Solomon Grundy.

Simple Simon

Simple Simon met a pieman,
Going to the fair;
Says Simple Simon to the pieman,
"Let me taste your ware."

Says the pieman to Simple Simon,
"Show me first your penny."
Says Simple Simon to the pieman,
"Indeed I have not any."

Simple Simon went a-fishing,
For to catch a whale;
All the water he had got
Was in his mother's pail.

Simple Simon went to look
If plums grew on a thistle;
He pricked his fingers very much,
Which made poor Simon whistle.

33

There Was An Old Woman

There was an old woman
  who lived in a shoe
She had so many children
  she didn't know what to do.
She gave them some broth
  without any bread.
She whipped them all soundly
  and put them to bed.

The Little Girl With A Curl

There was a little girl who had a little curl
Right in the middle of her forehead;
When she was good, she was very, very good,
And when she was bad, she was horrid.

35

Where Are You Going, My Pretty Maid

"Where are you going, my pretty maid?"
"I'm going a-milking, sir," she said.
"May I go with you, my pretty maid?"
"You're kindly welcome, sir," she said.
"Will you marry me, my pretty maid?"
"If it please you, kind sir," she said.

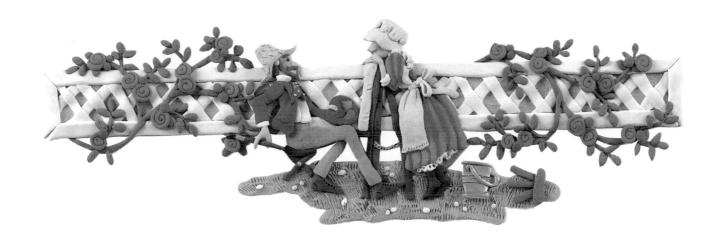

"What is your father, my pretty maid?"
"My father's a farmer, sir," she said.
"What is your fortune, my pretty maid?"
"My face is my fortune, sir," she said.
"Then I can't marry you, my pretty maid."
"Nobody asked you, sir," she said.

Rock-a-bye Baby

Rock-a-bye baby
On the treetop,
When the wind blows
The cradle will rock;
When the bough breaks
The cradle will fall,
And down will come cradle,
Baby, and all.

38

Tweedle-dum and Tweedle-dee

Tweedle-dum and Tweedle-dee
Resolved to have a battle,
For Tweedle-dum said Tweedle-dee
Had spoiled his nice new rattle.

Just then flew by a monstrous crow,
As big as a tar barrel,
Which frightened both the heroes so,
They quite forgot their quarrel.

To Market, To Market

To market, to market,
To buy a fat pig,
Home again, home again,
Jiggety-jig.
To market, to market,
To buy a fat hog,
Home again, home again,
Jiggety-jog.